2024 written by Sarah Surgey and Illustrated by Natasha Gunathilake
Sarah Surgey & Natasha Gunathilake are part of HB Publishing House.
All rights reserved. No part of this publication may be reproduced, stored in a retrieval system, or transmitted, in any form or in any means - by electronic, mechanical, photocopying, recording or otherwise - without prior written permission.
Jumping Hurdles
HB Publishing House, 21, NG13 7AW
British Library Catalogue in Publication Data: a catalogue record for this book is available from the British Library.
ISBN: 9781068642739

Jumping Hurdles

Written by Sarah Surgey

Illustrated by Natasha Gunathilake

The garden of 8-year-old Bea, was in chaos. She had built an obstacle course using as many items from her house as she could find. But now her mum was telling her it was time to tidy up, and Bea didn't want to.

She needed to keep practising for tomorrow!

"What's wrong?" asked mum.
"It's Sports Day tomorrow," Bea replied, "and I have to make sure that I win!"
"Try your best, remember it's not always about the winning, it's about showing up and showing who you are."

Bea smiled at her mum's words, she wanted to try her best, but realised that might not be good enough!

"You'll struggle with your co-ordination and balance," said the lady who had visited their house and chatted with her. She had called it Dyspraxia.

What a weird word!

She said that Dyspraxia is unique in each person. It can feel like you are telling your body to do one thing but sometimes your body might not listen.

So how would Bea win Sports Day if she had Dyspraxia?

Nope! She couldn't give up and needed to keep practising; her friends were relying on her.

But the following morning, Bea felt sick as if there were a lot of butterflies in her tummy.

Bea watched as one by one; her classmates picked their teams.

Bea was the last one left.

It didn't matter how many times this happened it still made her feel sad.

And she knew why!

Last year at sports day, she had fallen over and didn't win a single race for her team! Even her best friend Ruby didn't want to pick her now.

"Sorry, Bea," she said. "But I really want to win today."

Bea felt confused and her heart hurt.

This sports day was going to be the worst day ever!

After receiving their instructions, the teacher told them to head out onto the field.

Bea tried to remember some of the rules, but everything felt blurry. Instead, a wave of panic started to rise as she wondered what to do next.

The whistle blew, and all the children began to move to different spaces. How did they know where to go?
Is that what the teacher had been telling them this morning?

If she didn't do something quickly, she would end up in the wrong race!

"Where should I go?"

Bea's voice suddenly echoed out.

"You're doing the egg and spoon race", said a boy kindly.
"Oh. Thank you!" Bea replied.

Bea smiled with relief because she knew where that was! She had been curious to see the eggs when she walked past them earlier.

Bea held the spoon firmly in her hand, she noticed how differently her friends gripped theirs. But this was how she always held her cutlery and gripped her pen...

...different but strong!

The other children whizzed past her, soon their eggs started to fall off.
But Bea continued to walk slowly and carefully thinking about her every step.

There was the finishing line! Just a few more steps ...

"Second place! Well done!" said a lady with a clipboard at the end.

Bea felt really happy and proud of herself!

I am showing everybody who I am.

However, that feeling didn't last for long because the next race wasn't so easy.

This time, it was all about co-ordination and Bea knew that her Dyspraxia would make things a little more complicated.

She felt her heartbeat quicken and her palms became clammy.

She felt the panic rising again.

The whistle blew and Bea watched the other children run towards the assault course and climb under the net.

Bea followed closely behind... but she got into a muddle under the net and couldn't work out which way to go as the crowd's

    shouting

          grew

                louder!

The net felt like a never-ending tunnel.

She could feel the tears coming and closed her eyes to the thundering sounds of the crowd.

When suddenly, a warm hand held hers and she heard a voice. "Follow me!" it said softly.

Bea recognised her best friend, Ruby. "I'm sorry I didn't pick you earlier, but let me help you now."

Bea held her hand tightly and carried on.

And although Bea came last, she was so happy that she didn't give up!

Sports Day went on for a loooong time, but Bea kept on going.

She hated the relay race but loved the sack race!

All of her friends were falling all over the place and becoming quite frustrated, unlike Bea, who knew how to get back up quickly!

She was feeling good again until ... the whistle blew, and a teacher shouted, "Hurdles is the last race!"

Bea's tummy turned and she felt the butterflies take flight again.

She sighed unsure what to do. How would she be able to get her legs up and over the hurdles whilst running at the same time!

She stood staring at the obstacles until suddenly...

...it was time to go!

Bea ran to the first one and stopped.

Her team started shouting at her to jump.

Maybe she could jump without running?

Bea jumped as high as she could with both feet up.

She clipped the obstacle, which wobbled, but ...

...she was over!

The children started to cheer.

Feeling more confident, she ran to the next one and then stopped again.

With both feet, she did the same movement that she had used in the sack race.

This time, she fell, but like before, she got back up and felt determined to finish the race.

One by one, she saw other children sprint past her, but all Bea focused on was her hurdles.

It's not always about the winning.

Finally, she had made it to the last one. She slowed down, looked around and then ... OH NO!

Her friend Ruby was on the floor.

She had sprinted over so fast that she had crashed and fallen.

Bea's teammates shouted at her to keep going, but Ruby had helped her, and that's what friends were for.

"Get back up, Ruby!" Bea said, holding out her hand. "You might not win, but at least you'll finish."

Ruby took Bea's hand and got back up, "Let's run and finish together."

Bea was confused.

"But I know how much winning means to you," Bea said.

"Yes, but finishing together as friends, means more," Ruby smiled.

And as Bea crossed the finishing line, she felt

magical

and that maybe just being herself was

enough.

Her team came third, and that was good, thought Bea. She had completed all the races and helped her friend.

Yesterday, she hadn't known how she would jump over the hurdles.

But today, she found a way.

Maybe Dyspraxia made some things harder,

but if she focused on herself, and never gave up, the possibilities were endless!

Meet the Author

Sarah Surgey is a best-selling children's author. Her recent book 'The Heavy Bag' is translated into 16 different languages and is used in collaboration with UNICEF. Sarah has 4 books coming out in 2024, Jumping Hurdles will be the only book in the UK to feature a main character with Dyspraxia.

Sarah also edits and ghost writes for children's books whilst working as a freelance children's writer across Europe. Sarah has featured at The Bath Children's Literature Festival and holds writing courses for both children and adults.

Dyspraxia Support

If you or someone you know has a diagnosis of Dyspraxia, here are some places you can find support in the UK and Ireland.

Information, resources and support are available on the Dyspraxia/DCD website
www.dyspraxia.ie

The Brain Charity
www.thebraincharity.org.uk

Foundation for People with Learning Disabilities
www.learningdisabilities.org.uk

www.nhs.uk/conditions/developmental-coordination-disorder-dyspraxia-in-adults/

Let's be friends...

www.hbpublishinghouse.co.uk

- hb_publishing_house
- HB Publishing House
- hb_publishing_house

Draw a picture of you on Sports Day